The shark teeth we found
on the beach.
—Lottie

My Nana's handmade quilts.
—Maple

My Pokémon cards.
—Liam

A green string.
—Rosie

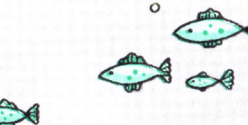

EMERALD

and the Lost Treasure

Harriet Muncaster

OXFORD
UNIVERSITY PRESS

For vampires, fairies, humans
and MERMAIDS everywhere!

Illustrated by Mike Love,
based on original artwork by Harriet Muncaster

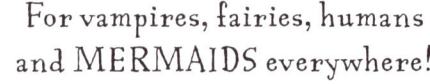

OXFORD
UNIVERSITY PRESS

Great Clarendon Street, Oxford OX2 6DP
Oxford University Press is a department of the University of Oxford.
It furthers the University's objective of excellence in research, scholarship,
and education by publishing worldwide. Oxford is a registered trade mark
of Oxford University Press in the UK and in certain other countries

British Library Cataloguing in Publication Data

Data available

ISBN: 978-0-19278401-8

1 3 5 7 9 10 8 6 4 2

Printed in China

The manufacturing process conforms to the
environmental regulations of the country of origin.

FSC
www.fsc.org

MIX
Paper | Supporting
responsible forestry
FSC® C020056

Scallop City

Town Hall

Marina's House

Finn's House

Park

Princess Delphina's School

Oceana's House

Emerald's Dad's House

Emerald's School

Palace

Family Tree

My Stepdad
King Auster

My Mum
Queen Coral

My Stepsister
Princess Delphina

Five reasons why you'll love Emerald...

Dive into a magical underwater kingdom!

Emerald's best friend is a little octopus called Inkibelle.

Emerald is learning about being a mermaid princess—but she's doing it *her* way.

Gorgeous green and black pictures.

Discover lost treasure!

What's your most treasured possession?

Barry, my pet snail.
—Esmerelda

A bangle from my dad.
—Poppy

My REAL pirate treasure!
(A marble and a coin we found
whilst planting the garden.)
—Riley

My family.
—Jessica

My Dad
Dace

My Dad's Girlfriend
Sirena

Inkibelle

Me!
Emerald

Chapter ONE

It was a bright morning under the sea, and I was eating breakfast as quickly as possible!

'I wish *my* school was going on a sea-combing expedition today!' grumbled my stepsister, Princess Delphina, as she ate her Kelp Krunchies.

'I'm sure you'll go sea-combing with your school too,' said my stepdad, King Auster. 'One day.'

Mum married Auster recently, so now I spend half my time in the palace and half my time with my dad in a small pearly pink house on the other side of Scallop City. It was hard to adjust at first, but I'm starting to quite like it.

'I'm so excited!' I squealed.

'Remember you're going to Dad's
house after school,' said Mum. 'I've packed
a bag for you—and one for Inkibelle—and
I also popped Starfish Plushie in too.'

'Thanks, Mum!'

Inkibelle is my pet octopus, and Starfish Plushie is my favourite cuddly toy. I swallowed the last of my Kelp Krunchies and whooshed up from my chair in a flurry of bubbles. I grabbed my bag, gave Mum and Auster a hug, and swooshed out of the door.

All my classmates were just as excited as me for the school trip.

'Last time I went sea-combing, I found a shiny golden coin!' said my friend Marina.

'And I found a *real* diamond!' added Finn.

'When I went with my dad last summer, I found a bracelet with green glass crystals,' I said. 'It's in my special jewellery box at his house. Maybe I'll find a matching necklace . . .'

Just then, Mrs Shell-Clacker came swimming into the classroom carrying an armful of fluorescent yellow *monstrosities.*

'Good morning, merpupils!' she said. 'Everyone will need to wear a hi-vis jacket for our sea-combing trip.'

She handed them round and I glowered at mine.

'You won't look like your punky self at all, Emerald!' giggled Marina.

I scowled. I don't like being told what to wear. I am proud of my very *specific* style. I like the colour black, loads of glitter, and everything gothic—and this jacket was none of that. Still, I *really* wanted to go sea-combing, so I reluctantly pulled it on.

Mrs Shell-Clacker clapped her hands
for attention. 'Today we will be combing
the ocean floor as part of our new
environmental project, *Finders Keepers*.
We'll swim through the magical deep and
up into the shallows where humans drop
most of their rubbish, and then we'll tidy
it up. Keeping our ocean floor clean is
vital for life down here, so when we arrive,
each of you will get a bag, a net, and a sea
spear.'

'Yeah! We get a sea spear!' yelled Finn
excitedly.

Mrs Shell-Clacker gave him a sharp
look.

'The sea spears are *not* for play
fighting with!' she said. '*Or* poking each
other with. Does everyone understand?'

'*Yes, Mrs Shell-Clacker,*' we all
chorused—including Finn.

'Very good. We will reuse or recycle
most things, but you will each keep one

item and write a story about it afterwards. If that's all clear, form up in two neat lines, and let's get going!'

We swam in our lines behind Mrs Shell-Clacker, turning away from the centre of Scallop City and out towards the magical deep. We soon stopped seeing so many houses and shops, and instead, the ocean floor grew wilder, teeming with fronds of waving seaweed and little scuttly creatures.

A large, silver shark glided by, and Mrs
Shell-Clacker gave it a pat on the head.
I gulped. All sea creatures are friendly
towards merpeople, but sharks still give
me the shivers!

Soon the water around us brightened to a light aqua colour, and far above, I could see the surface of the ocean rippling and twinkling. We were in shallow waters now—*human* waters—and the sandy floor was dotted with all kinds of unusual and colourful things. Finn darted down to poke something with his spear.

'What's this?!' he asked, waving a little box on the end of his spear.

'Please don't wave it around!' said Mrs Shell-Clacker, ducking out of the way. 'That is a juice box, Finn. Put it in your net, and we can bring it back for recycling.'

'It was so bright and orange, it looked

like treasure,' said Finn.

We all got to work, picking up rubbish and looking for treasures. Inkibelle swooshed along behind us in a sprinkling of inky bubbles.

'What's that?' asked Marina, pointing to something silvery billowing on the sandy floor. It looked like some sort of weird jellyfish!

'Oh,' said Marina despondently as we swam closer. 'It's just a plastic bag.'

'Not *just* a bag . . .' I peered inside and saw a tiny trapped amber crab. I shook him loose and he clicked his claws gratefully.

'Poor little thing!' I said as I stuffed the plastic bag into my net. 'Imagine if we hadn't been here to rescue him.'

Marina nodded just as a shriek came from somewhere nearby.

'*Mrs Shell-Clacker! Mrs Shell-Clacker! Looook!*'

We raced over to where our friend, Oceana, was happily bobbing about in the middle of a gathering crowd, holding out her hand for everyone to see. She was wearing a huge, sparkling, *real* ruby ring!

'Oh my!' said Mrs Shell-Clacker as she took Oceana's hand, gazing enviously at the beautiful ring. 'That really *is* treasure . . . Well done, Oceana. I'm sure you'll write a great story about it for the *Finders Keepers* project!'

I wished *I* had found a ruby ring! I knew exactly the kind of story I would write about such a sparkling treasure. It would involve pirates and shipwrecks and magic!

'Maybe there's more jewellery around,' said Marina hopefully. 'Let's look! Come on, Emerald!'

I found a human shoe covered in barnacles and a pair of broken spectacles, which I put in my net. I was carefully peering into a half-open clam shell to see if there was a pearl inside when Marina tugged at my arm.

'What's that?' she asked, pointing at a clump of jewel-green seaweed nearby.

There was an unusual lumpy shape nestled inside, so we swam over for a closer look.

'Oh,' said Marina, sounding disappointed. 'It's just a teddy bear!'

'A *cute* teddy bear!' I said, snatching it up and hugging it to my chest.

'Well, you can have it if you want,' said Marina, shrugging.

I held the teddy bear out in front of me. He had caramel-coloured fur and shiny black button eyes. There was writing sewn into its leather label:

MY NAME IS: BERTIE

I BELONG TO: JACK

IF LOST, PLEASE RETURN ME TO:

SCALLOP BAY LIGHTHOUSE

'Are you going to keep it for the project?' asked Marina.

'I can't keep him,' I replied. 'He belongs to someone else!'

'But you know it's not possible for merpeople to return lost things to humans,' said Marina. 'It's finders-keepers under the sea, so that bear is yours now, Emerald! Well, *technically* mine as I found it. But I don't mind. I bet you could make up a great story about it for the project!'

I gazed at the teddy bear, wondering if Jack was missing Bertie. I couldn't help thinking of my own very special starfish plushie. I sleep with her every night, and I would be *so* upset if she ever went missing! I've had Starfish Plushie since I was a tiny mer-baby.

I hugged the teddy bear close.

'I'll look after you now, Bertie,' I whispered.

It felt like a long swim back to Mrs Shell-Clacker's Academy at the end of the day, especially now that we were all weighed down with bags full of litter! Marina swished along beside me in a flurry of bubbles. She was pleased because she had finally found some treasure—a pretty hairclip with a rainbow on it.

'I wish we had rainbows under the sea!' she said. 'I've only ever seen pictures of them in books.'

'Me too,' I agreed. 'I'd *love* to see a real one!'

When we arrived back at school, Mrs
Shell-Clacker told us to drop our litter
bags in a great big pile outside.

'Well done, everyone,' she said to the
class. 'We'll sort all this out next week.
You've made a real difference today.'

'Can we take our treasures home?'
asked Marina hopefully, touching the
rainbow clip in her hair. I clutched Bertie
tight. I didn't like the idea of leaving him
in an empty, dark school over the weekend.

'You may,' said Mrs Shell-Clacker. I breathed a sigh of relief. 'But make sure you bring them back to school next week so you can write your stories.'

'Do you want to come to mine for dinner?' I asked Marina as we set off for home. 'We usually have pasta shells with sauce on a Friday.'

'Ooh, yes please!' said Marina. 'We'll just have to swim by my house on the way to let my mum know.'

Chapter TWO

'Hi, Dad!' I yelled, pushing open the
front door and swooshing through to the
kitchen with Marina and Inkibelle.

'Emerald!' Dad exclaimed, opening
his arms for a big hug. 'And it's nice to see
you too, Marina. Would you like to stay
for dinner?'

'Yes, please!' replied Marina. 'I

already checked
with my mum,
and she said it
was OK.'

'Hello, you
two!' smiled Sirena,
swimming into the kitchen.
Sirena is my dad's girlfriend. I didn't like
her at first, but now I think she's *lovely*!

Marina and I went to my bedroom
to play before dinner. I pulled Starfish
Plushie out of my bag and
propped her against
the pillow, then
carefully sat Bertie
next to her.

A teddy looked a bit out of place among all the other sea creature toys and ornaments in my bedroom.

'Do you want to make bracelets?' I asked Marina. 'I've got some new pearls in pink and green. They're so shimmery!'

'Ooh, yes!' said Marina. So I got the beads out and we sat together for a while by the window, threading beads onto string and watching the colourful fish that swam by. My bracelet was going to be a little one for Bertie Bear. My gaze kept drifting over to him. His fur was all fuzzy in the water! He was so cute. But I was sure that his button eyes looked just a little bit sad.

'Do you think he's missing Jack?' I asked.

'Who?' asked Marina.

'The bear! He must be missing his human! *Jack* must be missing *Bertie*!'

'Oh,' said Marina. 'Well, maybe. But I don't think you should worry about it. You know the rules of the sea—whatever lands down here is ours to keep.'

'I know,' I said, but I didn't feel sure. There was something about Bertie being here that didn't feel *right*.

'I wonder if there's a way to get him back to Jack . . .' I said.

'What?!' Marina stopped threading beads and stared at me, shocked. 'Jack is a human who lives on land, and we're mermaids! It's not possible!'

'Isn't it?' I said, as a brilliant and exciting idea suddenly fell into my head. 'All we need is a human to help us, Marina! *You* know someone who lives on land. Isadora Moon! She came to your birthday sleepover.'

'Isadora Moon!' said Marina, her eyes suddenly lighting up. 'Oh, I haven't seen her in ages! I didn't even think of that! She's not technically a human, you know. She's a vampire fairy.'

'Even better!' I said. 'She has magic. I'm sure she could help us!'

Marina's tail began to twitch with excitement.

'It *would* be an adventure!' she said.

'Let's write Isadora a letter right now!' I said. 'We can send it by seagull.'

'OK,' agreed Marina. 'We'll ask Isadora to come to Scallop Bay at the weekend. We can swim up to the shore and give her the bear, then hopefully, she'll be able to find Jack and return it.'

I nodded, trying to ignore the twinge of sadness I got from the thought of saying goodbye to Bertie.

'If Isadora can't find Jack,' said

Marina, 'then you can keep him. And you won't feel guilty about it because you'll know we did our best to find his owner. And he has the best possible *new* owner.'

'OK,' I agreed, glancing over at Bertie again before starting on the letter. 'It's all we can do.'

DEAR ISADORA,

WE NEED YOUR HELP! MARINA AND I HAVE FOUND A TEDDY CALLED BERTIE. HE BELONGS TO SOMEONE CALLED JACK, AND THEY LIVE AT SCALLOP BAY LIGHTHOUSE. CAN YOU HELP US RETURN BERTIE TO HIM? IF SO, PLEASE MEET US AT THE SCALLOP BAY ROCKPOOLS AT TEN O'CLOCK ON SUNDAY MORNING!

LOVE FROM EMERALD AND MARINA X

By the time we had sealed up the envelope and written the address in waterproof mermaid ink, it was dinner time. We swished down to the kitchen and gobbled up pasta shells with sauce and sea fruit trifle as fast as we could.

'In a hurry?' laughed Dad.

As soon as we had finished eating,

Marina and I swam out of the house
and up, up, up through the sapphire blue
waters of the sea towards the surface. We
popped our heads out of the water in a
sprinkling of salt water, sparkling gold
in the evening light. Marina squinted at
the sky and waved at a flock of squawking
seagulls.

'There!' she said. 'Splash around, Emerald!'

Together we lay back in the water and waved and splashed our tails over and over until a seagull noticed us and flew down.

'Please can you take this letter to our friend, Isadora Moon?' I asked. The seagull tilted its head in a listening sort of way as we told it Isadora's full address.

When we had finished, the seagull nodded and said 'Squawk!', holding out its foot as we tied on the letter.

'Thank you!' said Marina. 'You're very kind!'

The seagull squawked again—as if to say *yes, I am*!—then rose up into the sky and flapped off into the sunset.

Chapter THREE

On Sunday morning, Marina and I swam
as fast as we could through the water
towards Scallop Bay, flurries of bubbles
trailing out behind us. Bertie was tucked
safely in my rucksack. We were both *so*
excited! Our parents had said we could
stay out all day as long as Isadora's
parents were at the beach.

'We're almost there!' said Marina. 'I *so* hope Isadora got the letter!'

'Me too,' I said, starting to feel a bit worried that all our excitement might be for nothing.

As we swooshed along, I could see the sunlight starting to pierce through the surface of the sea in wavy rays.

'We're near the Scallop Bay rockpools now,' said Marina, and we poked our heads out of the ocean.

'There's Isadora and her family!' I gasped. 'They came!'

'Yay!' whooped Marina. 'And there's no one else around. That's good.'

It was exciting to be so close to land. Marina and I swam on until we were right among the fluffy white waves crashing on the shoreline.

'Isadora!' cried Marina, waving her arms about.

A figure on the beach in a black and white striped swimming costume turned towards us.

'Marina!' Isadora yelled. 'Emerald!'

She ran across the sand and splashed into the sea, followed by Pink Rabbit and a taller girl who was staring at us with her mouth open.

'This is my cousin, Mirabelle!' said Isadora as the four of us bobbed among the waves at waist height. 'She's half-witch, half-fairy. She's staying with us for the weekend! And do you remember Pink Rabbit? He was my favourite stuffed toy, but my mum magicked him alive with her fairy wand!'

'Hello, Mirabelle,' I said. 'I've never met a real half-witch half-fairy before!'

'I've never met a mermaid before!' said Mirabelle. 'I love your shimmery tail. I bet you can swim super fast! What's it like living under the water? I bet sharks are always trying to eat you, aren't they?'

Marina and I laughed. 'Sharks are OK really,' I said, shrugging.

'This must be Bertie,' said Isadora.

I held Bertie up. He was still wearing the pearl bracelet I had made for him. I gave him a squeeze and rubbed my cheek on his soft fur, then I handed him over to Isadora. She read the leather label. '*Scallop Bay Lighthouse,*' she said. 'We're already in Scallop Bay, so the lighthouse must be somewhere nearby.'

46

We gazed around at the beach and the cliffs. I couldn't see any sort of lighthouse anywhere.

'Mum and Dad might know where it is,' said Isadora.

I bit my lip. What if Isadora and Mirabelle couldn't find Jack? Or worse, what if they made a mistake and gave Bertie Bear to the wrong person?

'If you can't find Jack, I'm happy to take Bertie home with me!' I said quickly. 'Maybe you could bring him back here tomorrow if you don't have any luck?'

'I wish we were able to come with you,' cried Marina. 'It would be so much fun to explore on land!'

'I wish you were able to come and help too,' said Isadora. 'Isn't there some kind of mermaid magic that you could use?'

Marina shook her head. 'Mermaids have to stay in the water. It's the only place we can move with our tails.'

Isadora looked disappointed, but I noticed that Mirabelle's eyes had gone a little bit glinty.

'*I* have an idea,' Mirabelle said. 'I'm great at shrinking potions! I've used them

loads. I could make you into *teeny tiny* mermaids, small enough to fit in a bucket of water! Then Isadora and I could carry you to the lighthouse.'

I felt my heart pitter-patter with excitement, but Isadora looked unsure.

'Your shrinking potions always get us into trouble . . .' she said.

'I promise it won't this time,' said Mirabelle. 'Oh, come on, Isadora! It would be so much fun.'

'I want to do it!' burst out Marina, clasping her hands together. 'Our parents aren't expecting us back for ages, and being a tiny mermaid sounds *wonderful*.'

'It *would* be an adventure to leave the ocean for a while,' I agreed.

Isadora sighed. 'I guess it might be OK . . . as long as you *promise*, Mirabelle, not to get us into any trouble!'

Mirabelle grinned and fiddled with her potion bottle necklace.

'Shrinking potions are my favourite,' she said gleefully. She took the stopper off one of the tiny bottles and poured a heap of pink glittering powder into an upturned clam shell. Then she leaned forward and blew it all over Marina and *POOF*! She shrunk to the size of an oyster and plopped down into the shallows. Isadora immediately scooped her up before she got swept away.

'Your turn, Emerald!' said Mirabelle, taking Bertie from me so that he didn't shrink too, though I would've liked time to kiss him goodbye. She blew the glittering powder all over me and suddenly my fins began to tingle and everything sparkled.

POOF!

The world grew
big around me, and
Isadora and Mirabelle shot up
like giants! I fell what felt like a thousand
miles down into the water with a splash
before Isadora's huge hand came towards
me lifting me out of the sea and up into
the air. It was a *very* strange feeling.

'I'll go and
fetch a bucket!' said
Mirabelle, and she splashed
her way out of the water and ran up the
beach, coming back a minute later with
a green plastic bucket. It felt refreshing
to be dropped back into the water again.
Mermaid tails don't like getting too dry.

'Let's go and find Jack!' said Isadora,
her voice booming above us.

Chapter FOUR

It felt funny to be riding along in a bucket. It was very . . . swingy. Marina and I popped our heads over the rim while Isadora and Mirabelle carried us up the beach to Isadora's family.

'Collecting shells is my sister's favourite thing to do,'

said Isadora on the way. 'Her name is Honeyblossom.'

Honeyblossom looked up when we got close and spotted Marina and me peering over the edge of the bucket. We waved to her and she laughed excitedly, dropping her dummy out of her mouth onto the sand.

'What is it, Honeyblossom?' asked Isadora's mum, Countess Cordelia. She had long pink hair and shimmery fairy wings. She looked to where Honeyblossom was pointing. 'Oh!' she said, peering down at the bucket. 'Is that you, Marina? And another mermaid too, I see. You're both… *tiny*!'

'It's alright, Aunt Cordelia,' said Mirabelle, turning red. 'We won't cause any trouble this time, I *promise*! Marina and Emerald wanted to help us return Bertie.'

'Yes, we really *want* to come!' Marina and I squeaked from the bucket.

'Isadora told us about your plans,'

said Isadora's dad, Count Bartholomew.
He was wearing a large pair of sunglasses,
a thick vampire cape, and holding a pointy
parasol above his head to shield himself
from the sun. 'A very kind thing to do.'

'We need to find Scallop Bay
Lighthouse,' Isadora said. 'That's where
Bertie's owner lives.'

'I think the
lighthouse is
just over the
sand dunes,'
said Cordelia,
pointing that
way. 'I can help
you find it.'

'It's OK, Aunt Cordelia,' said Mirabelle sweetly. 'We can go ourselves.'

'I'm not sure about that!' said Bartholomew. 'Mischief just seems to follow you around, Mirabelle. Aunt Cordelia will go with you while I stay and look after Honeyblossom.'

'I'm sure it won't take long,' said Cordelia. 'We'll be back for the picnic

soon. Come along, my sugarplums. Let's
find the lighthouse!'

We all waved goodbye to Count
Bartholomew and Honeyblossom and
ventured off towards the dunes with
Bertie Bear in Mirabelle's backpack.
Marina and I continued to poke our heads
above the rim of the bucket.

'I'll carry them for a bit if you like!' offered Mirabelle. Isadora handed the bucket to Mirabelle, and the two of them followed Cordelia climbing up the sand dunes. They were very steep, and Mirabelle was not as gentle with the bucket as Isadora! Marina and I held onto the rim for dear life as we swung back and forth, water sloshing out everywhere. It made me feel a bit sick.

'MIIIRAAABEELLE!' we yelled as loudly as we could. 'GIVE US BACK TO ISADOORAAA!'

When we got to the top of the sand
dunes, Isadora, Mirabelle, and Cordelia
stopped for a moment and Marina and I
gasped. We had never seen the sea from so
high up before.

'Wow!' said Marina in awe. '*That's*
where we live . . .'

'It's so big and blue and shiny!' I said.
'It looks like it goes on *forever*!'

Then Isadora moved the bucket round so that we were facing inland, and we gasped again. There was no sea at all! No twinkly blue! Just brown and green and grey, going on for miles and miles and miles. There were box-like buildings dotted everywhere with roads between them like wiggly grey eels.

'So weird,' I said.

'*So* weird,' agreed Marina.

I swished around, searching in all directions.

'Look over there!' I cried.

On the edge of a cliff, at the far end of a thin and sandy path, stood a tall tower with red and white stripes going

all the way up. It *had* to be the lighthouse!
I gripped onto the edge of the bucket,
peering out eagerly, as Mirabelle, Isadora,
and Cordelia headed straight towards it.
When we got closer, I could see a boy
sitting outside on the rocks and a man on
the shore nearby.

'That must be the lighthouse keeper!'
said Cordelia, and she hurried off to talk
to him.

Isadora and Mirabelle walked
towards the boy sitting on the rocks. He
was gazing out to sea through a pair of
binoculars and noting things down in a
book.

'Do you think that's Jack?' Marina
asked me.

'Maybe . . .' I said, half-hoping it
wasn't so I might keep Bertie Bear for
myself.

'Hi!' said Mirabelle, waving at the
boy. Isadora followed, walking more
carefully so as not to spill us out of

the bucket. Marina and I ducked down beneath the rim, but we couldn't resist peeping our heads back up again. We had never seen a human so close before!

The boy had green glasses and a friendly smile, but he looked very surprised.

'Are you a . . . *vampire*?' he asked Isadora. 'You've got fangs and . . . and . . . bat wings! Wow!'

'I'm a vampire fairy actually,' replied Isadora, proudly. 'And this is my witch fairy cousin, Mirabelle.'

'Is your name Jack?' asked Mirabelle. 'And have you lost a teddy bear?'

The boy's face brightened with hope.

'I *am* Jack!' he said. 'And, yes, I *have* lost a bear! My favourite bear. He's called Bertie! I was out in the fishing boat with my dad the other day, and I *shouldn't* have taken Bertie, but I did anyway, and the waves got rough, and he fell overboard. I miss him more than anything!'

Mirabelle took Bertie Bear out of her backpack and held it out towards Jack. He gasped, and his eyes filled with tears. He grabbed Bertie and hugged him tightly, even though he was still soaking wet from the sea. He was still wearing the pearl bracelet, and I felt my heart twinge.

Jack gazed at Mirabelle and Isadora, his eyes shining.

'Thank you!' he cried. 'Thank you so much! But I don't understand . . . *how*?

I dropped Bertie out at sea. I thought he was lost forever!'

I saw Isadora and Mirabelle look at each other.

'Er…' began Isadora.

But before either of them could say anything else, Marina suddenly leapt up from the bucket, doing a little somersault and landing with a splash back in the water.

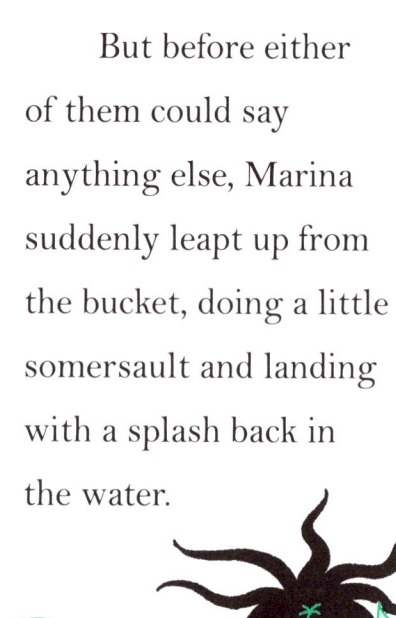

'I found him!' she shouted in her tiny little voice. 'It was meee!'

I saw Jack's eyes go big and round. He stepped forward to peer into the bucket. I shrank back as his big face loomed down.

'Is that…?' he stuttered. 'Are those…?'

'Er, mermaids, yes,' said Mirabelle.

'*Tiny* mermaids!' gasped Jack, astonished. 'I often look through my binoculars hoping to see a mermaid— although I did think they'd be bigger, I suppose—and now here are *two*! This is the best day ever!'

He stared down at us both with his huge eyes.

'How did you find Bertie?' he asked.

'He was caught in a clump of seaweed,' said Marina. '*I* found him, but it was Emerald's idea to try and find you and give him back. That's Emerald, by the way, and I'm Marina.'

Jack smiled down at me. 'Did you give Bertie this bracelet?' he asked inspecting the bracelet around Bertie's arm.

I nodded.

'I love it,' he said. 'And I know he does as well. Thank you, Emerald, and thank you too, Marina!'

'That's OK,' I said and shrugged,

pretending that I didn't care all that much about saying goodbye to Bertie. 'I have a special cuddly toy too. I don't know what I'd do if I lost it!'

'What toy do you have?' asked Jack. 'Is it a sea creature? Are you friends with all the real sea animals? I have so many questions! I want to know all about your underwater world!'

Marina laughed.

'Emerald is a *princess* of the underwater world!' she said proudly.

'Really!?' Jack looked astonished. 'You're a princess?'

He blushed and then bowed.

I felt my own face turn red.

'Oh, you don't have to bow to me!'
I said. 'I'm nothing like a usual kind of
princess. I just do my own thing, my own
way.'

'That's what I like to do too!' said
Jack, grinning.

'Do you really live in that tall stripy
tube?' interrupted Marina, pointing at the
lighthouse.

'That's where I live with my dad,'
said Jack. 'He's the lighthouse keeper.' He
pointed down at the shore where his dad
was chatting to Cordelia. 'He's fixing our
boat today. Do you want to come inside
and look around?'

'YES PLEASE!!' we shouted.

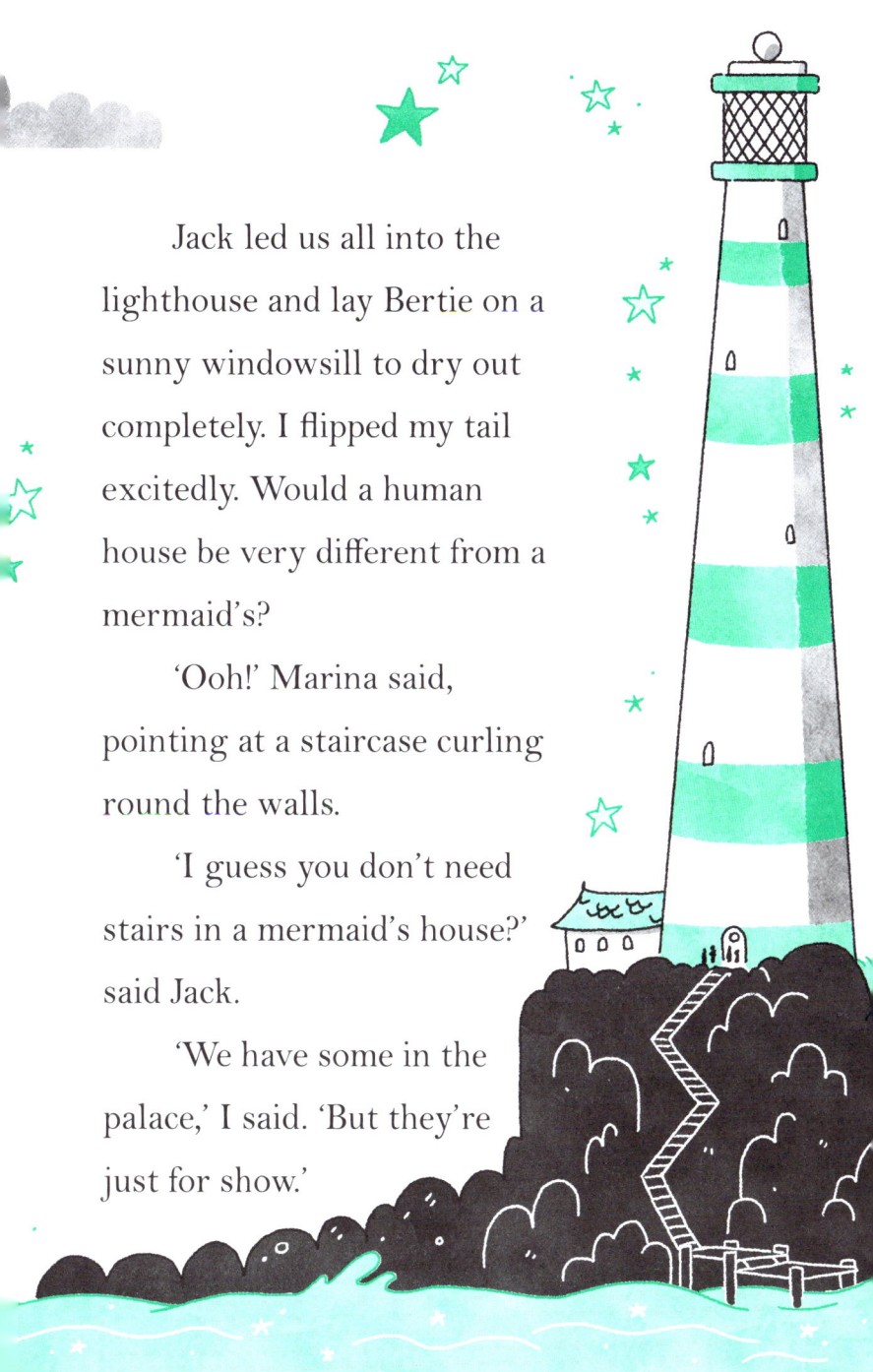

Jack led us all into the lighthouse and lay Bertie on a sunny windowsill to dry out completely. I flipped my tail excitedly. Would a human house be very different from a mermaid's?

'Ooh!' Marina said, pointing at a staircase curling round the walls.

'I guess you don't need stairs in a mermaid's house?' said Jack.

'We have some in the palace,' I said. 'But they're just for show.'

Being carried up the spiral staircase made me and Marina feel dizzy! Jack showed us his bedroom. There were colourful maps and pictures pinned all over the walls and glow stars sprinkled across the ceiling. There was a telescope in front of the window, and beneath the window sill, there was a shelf heaving with books about the sea and animals and the night sky. Best of all, there was a big glass case with water in it next to Jack's bed. It was full of brightly coloured plants and fish and even a castle!

'You have some of the ocean in your bedroom,' I said, smiling.

'That's my aquarium,' said Jack. 'I love everything to do with the sea.'

'Can we have a swim in it? I could do with stretching my tail!'

'Sure!' said Jack, and he carried the bucket over to the aquarium, tipping it slightly so that we could both splish down into the water.

Marina and I swam round and round and round, weaving in and out of the seaweed, looping the loop, and exploring the model castle.

'Did you see all of Jack's books about the ocean?' asked Marina. 'It's amazing to think that some humans love the sea as much as we do.'

Eventually, Jack came back over to the aquarium holding a sketchpad and pencil. Marina and I popped our heads above the water so that we could talk to him.

'Do you mind if I draw you?' Jack asked.

'Of course!' I said and tried my best to strike a pose. Jack put his head down and concentrated for a while. Scritch, scritch, scritch went his pencil.

'There!' he said at last, holding up

the sketchpad for us to see. Jack had drawn a beautiful, dreamlike picture of Marina and me swimming, our hair flowing out behind us.

'Oh, that's so good!' said Isadora coming over to look. 'You're brilliant at drawing, Jack.'

Jack shrugged. 'I practise a lot,' he said. 'It gets lonely here sometimes. There's not a lot of other children around for me to play with, and Dad's often busy.'

'Oh,' said Isadora, looking a bit sad.

'Well, I know! Would you and your dad like to come back to the beach with us for a picnic? Mum and Dad always pack loads of food. My mum's a fairy anyway; she could always magic more food up!'

Jack's eyes sparkled.

'I'd *love* that!' he said. 'I'll bring Bertie too, of course! He loves picnics!'

Chapter FIVE

That afternoon, we all sat on the beach
together with Isadora's family, Jack, and
his dad, and had a picnic. Marina and I
sat on the rim of the bucket, dangling our
tails into the water. I watched as Jack sat
with Bertie on his lap, so happy to have his
bear back. I still felt a bit sad about saying
goodbye to Bertie, but I knew that we had

done the right thing.

Isadora and Mirabelle kept passing us pieces of food to eat.

'This is a strawberry,' said Isadora, holding a big red fruit out towards me.

'Oof!' I said, wrapping my arms around it. 'It's heavy! But it smells so *sweet*!'

Love Emerald?
Why not try these too...

Harriet Muncaster, that's me! I'm the
creator of three young fiction series,
Isadora Moon, Mirabelle, and Emerald,
as well as the Victoria Stitch series for
older readers. I love anything teeny tiny,
anything starry, and everything glittery.

To visit
Harriet Muncaster's
website, go to
harrietmuncaster.co.uk

MIRABELLE

From the world of ISADORA MOON
MIRABELLE
Gets up to Mischief
Half witch, half fairy, totally naughty!
Harriet Muncaster

From the world of ISADORA MOON
MIRABELLE
and the Naughty Bat Kittens
Half witch, half fairy, totally naughty!
Harriet Muncaster

From the world of ISADORA MOON
MIRABELLE
and the Midnight Feast
Half witch, half fairy, totally naughty!
Harriet Muncaster

From the world of ISADORA MOON
MIRABELLE
Wants to Win
Half witch, half fairy, totally naughty!
Harriet Muncaster

From the world of ISADORA MOON
MIRABELLE
Has a Bad Day
Half witch, half fairy, totally naughty!
Harriet Muncaster

ISADORA MOON
Meets the Tooth Fairy

Half vampire, half fairy, totally unique!
Harriet Muncaster

ISADORA MOON
and the Shooting Star

Half vampire, half fairy, totally unique!
Harriet Muncaster

ISADORA MOON
Under the Sea
Half vampire, half fairy, totally unique!
Harriet Muncaster

ISADORA MOON

Gets the Magic Pox

Half vampire, half fairy, totally unique!
Harriet Muncaster

ISADORA MOON

and the New Girl

Half vampire, half fairy, totally unique!
Harriet Muncaster

ISADORA MOON

Has a Sleepover

Half vampire, half fairy, totally unique!

Harriet Muncaster

ISADORA MOON

Puts on a Show

Half vampire, half fairy, totally unique!

Harriet Muncaster

ISADORA MOON

and the Frost Festival

Half vampire, half fairy, totally unique!

Plus Isadorable activities!

Harriet Muncaster

ISADORA MOON

Goes on Holiday

Half vampire, half fairy, totally unique!

Harriet Muncaster

ISADORA MOON

Goes to a Wedding

Half vampire, half fairy, totally unique!

Harriet Muncaster

ISADORA MOON

Makes Winter Magic

Half vampire, half fairy, totally
Harriet Muncaster

ISADORA MOON

Goes to the Fair

vampire, half fairy, totally unique!
Harriet Muncaster

ISADORA MOON

Helps Out

Half vampire, half fairy, totally unique!
Harriet Muncaster

ISADORA MOON

Goes on a School Trip

Half vampire, half fairy, totally unique!
Harriet Muncaster

ISADORA MOON

Gets in Trouble

Half vampire, half fairy, totally unique!
Harriet Muncaster

ISADORA · MOON

ISADORA · MOON
Goes to School
Half vampire, half fairy, totally unique!
Harriet Muncaster

ISADORA · MOON
Goes Camping
Half vampire, half fairy, totally unique!
Harriet Muncaster

ISADORA · MOON
Has a Birthday
Half vampire, half fairy, totally unique!
Harriet Muncaster

ISADORA · MOON
Goes to the Ballet
Half vampire, half fairy, totally unique!
Harriet Muncaster

Method:

1. Cut strips in the bottom of your cardboard tube and fold them outwards to make the octopus legs. You can make these longer by sticking cardboard strips on the end of each tentacle.

2. Paint or colour in the cardboard and add a smiley face!

Make your very own Inkibelle

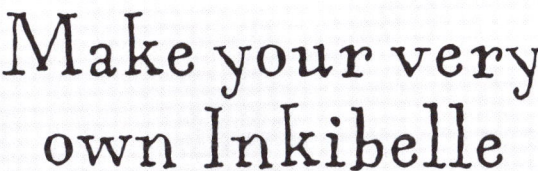

Emerald and her friends reuse or recycle the
rubbish they find on the ocean floor.
You can make some brilliant art
with everyday rubbish too!

You will need:

- a toilet roll or kitchen roll tube
- a pair of scissors
- cardboard for cutting into strips
- paint or pens

Write a poem about your favourite place.

Make something cool out of rubbish.

Do something helpful for someone else.

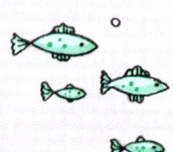

Message in a bottle

Write messages to your future self!

All you need is a glass jar or bottle, paper, and pens. Cut the paper into strips and write a little note to yourself or an idea for something fun to do on a rainy day.

Here are some ideas:

Draw a picture of your favourite sea creature.

3. I like my friends because ...

A. They are always up for an adventure.

B. They help me out when I need it.

C. They are kind and fun.

Mostly Cs
You would make a great vampire fairy! You are a great friend and you are kind and helpful.

Mostly Bs
You are a brilliant, unique human! You're thoughtful and artistic.

Mostly As
You would make a great merperson! You love the water and are always up for an exciting adventure.

Results

Quiz

Which character are you?
Take the quiz and find out!

1. What is your favourite thing to do at the weekend?

A. You love water, so your favourite thing to do is to go swimming — jumping in and splashing about is the best.

B. Reading all your favourite books about the ocean and all the amazing creatures who live there.

C. You love astronomy and the dark, starry night, so you like staying up late and looking at the stars.

2. What would your favourite cuddly toy look like?

A. A starfish plushie

B. A teddy bear

C. A pink rabbit!

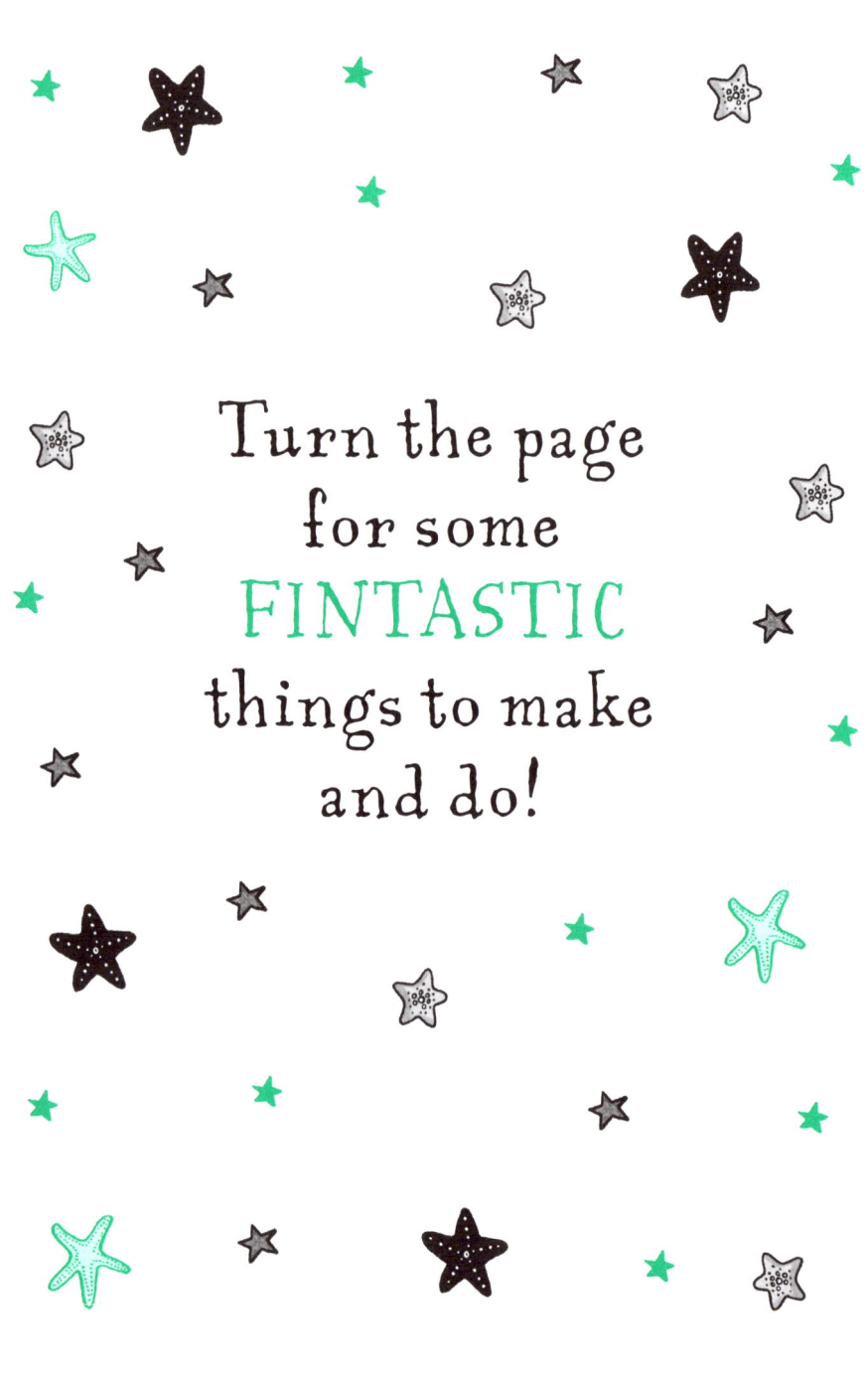

Turn the page
for some
FINTASTIC
things to make
and do!

I laughed and wondered if Mrs Shell-Clacker would believe any of it was true. But then, I thought, *I know it's all true, and that's really all that matters.*

It turned out that Bertie Bear—and Jack's big smile—had been the best treasures of all!

'Oh, it's so beautiful!' sighed Marina.

The sea was always amazing, but I'd never guessed land could be so magical too.

We gazed at the rainbow until it faded into the sky, then dipped our heads back down beneath the glittering waves, heading towards home, side by side. I didn't have Bertie with me anymore, but I had something better: new friends and the memories of a magical day in the sunshine. My heart felt full.

'You're going to be able to write such an amazing story about Bertie Bear for the *Finders Keepers* project!' said Marina. 'And you won't even have to make it up!'

special little wave to
Bertie.

'I'm glad you made it home,
Bertie,' I whispered. 'I'll miss you.'

Then Marina and I turned away
from them all and faced out to sea. It had
started raining again, the drops rippling
across the pink and gold water.

'Oh, my goodness!' gasped Marina
suddenly, pointing at the sky. I looked up
and gasped too.

'A *rainbow*!' we
both cried. 'A real
one!'

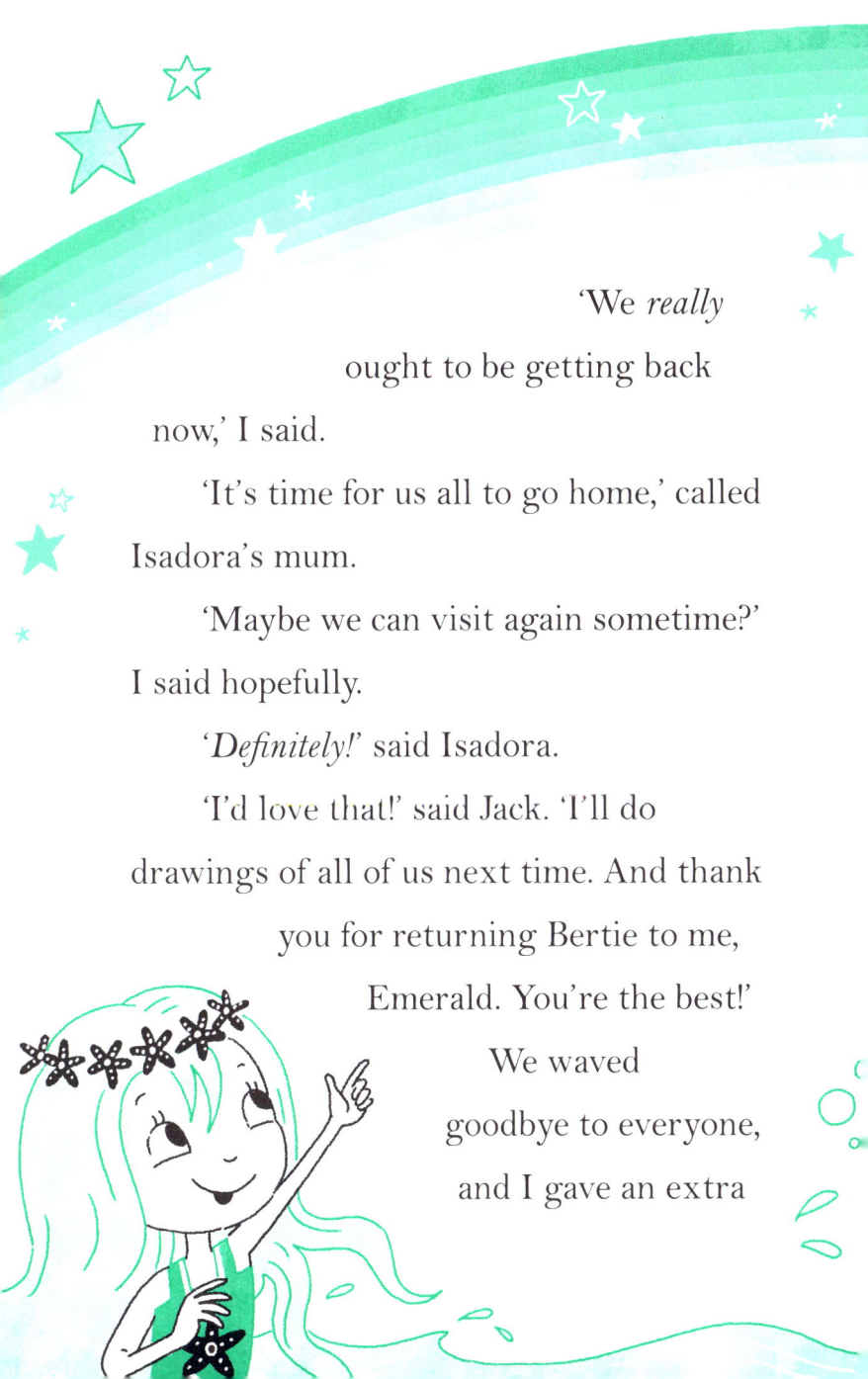

'We *really*
ought to be getting back
now,' I said.

'It's time for us all to go home,' called
Isadora's mum.

'Maybe we can visit again sometime?'
I said hopefully.

'*Definitely!*' said Isadora.

'I'd love that!' said Jack. 'I'll do
drawings of all of us next time. And thank
you for returning Bertie to me,
Emerald. You're the best!'

We waved
goodbye to everyone,
and I gave an extra

'Got you!' cried Jack, tapping me on the shoulder. 'You're *it* now!

We carried on playing for a little while longer until the sun began to dip towards the horizon.

I grabbed it from the seabed and held it
up, dripping.

'Honeyblossom!' I cried. 'Look!'

I threw the shell through the air
towards Cordelia, who flapped up on her
fairy wings to catch it. Honeyblossom
took it and grinned happily.

Both of us flopped gratefully back into the ocean. It felt SO good to be back in the salty seawater!

'OK!' said Mirabelle, splashing into the waves. 'You're *it*, Jack.'

Jack ran in, chasing me and Marina and Isadora while Isadora's parents stood on the sand with Honeyblossom and chatted to Jack's dad. I plunged beneath the waves and whooshed away from Jack, enjoying the cool water, when something caught my eye: a big, beautiful shell that shone with all the colours of the rainbow!

and took the stopper off the tiny bottle of shrinking potion. She poured a little bit into the upturned clam shell in the palm of her hand.

POOF!

She blew the pink glittering powder all over me. And then all over Marina. There was a fizz and a sparkle and suddenly we sprang right out of the bucket, growing to our normal size.

'We should probably start packing up,' he said. 'It's getting late, and rain does nothing for sleek vampire hair-dos.'

Isadora, Mirabelle, and Jack looked disappointed.

'Isn't there time for just one game?' asked Mirabelle. 'We could play sea tag.'

'I suppose rain doesn't matter if you're playing in the sea!' said Cordelia cheerfully.

'Let's play *one* quick game of tag,' I said. 'And then Marina and I ought to be getting home too.'

Isadora picked up the bucket and walked us down to the water's edge. Mirabelle reached for her necklace again

Once we'd finished the sandwiches
and fruit, Countess Cordelia produced
a huge cake with swirls of buttercream
and cherries. We munched it down while
Honeyblossom crawled about looking for
more shells, and by the time everything
had been eaten, a few drops of light rain
were beginning to sprinkle from the
afternoon sky, glimmering in the sunshine.

'Ooh!' squealed Marina. '*Rain!* We
don't get rain under the sea!'

Bartholomew looked
up at the sky, worried.

'Try this!' said Mirabelle, holding out a crumb from her sandwich. 'It's peanut butter!'

'*Peanut butter?*' I said, taking a small lick. '*Mmm!*'

'Peanut butter sandwiches are *my* absolute favourite!' said Isadora.

'Oh, mine too!' said Jack happily.

'*I* prefer red juice,' said Count Bartholomew as he slurped some through a straw. 'Would you like to try some, Emerald and Marina? I've got plenty— and there's nothing quite as delicious and nutritious for a vampire!'

Marina and I glanced at each other. 'That's OK, Mr Moon,' we said.

I took a bite from the giant strawberry, and Marina took a bite from the other side.

'Yum!' we both said.

'This strawberry tastes quite different from the ones we have under the sea,' said Marina.